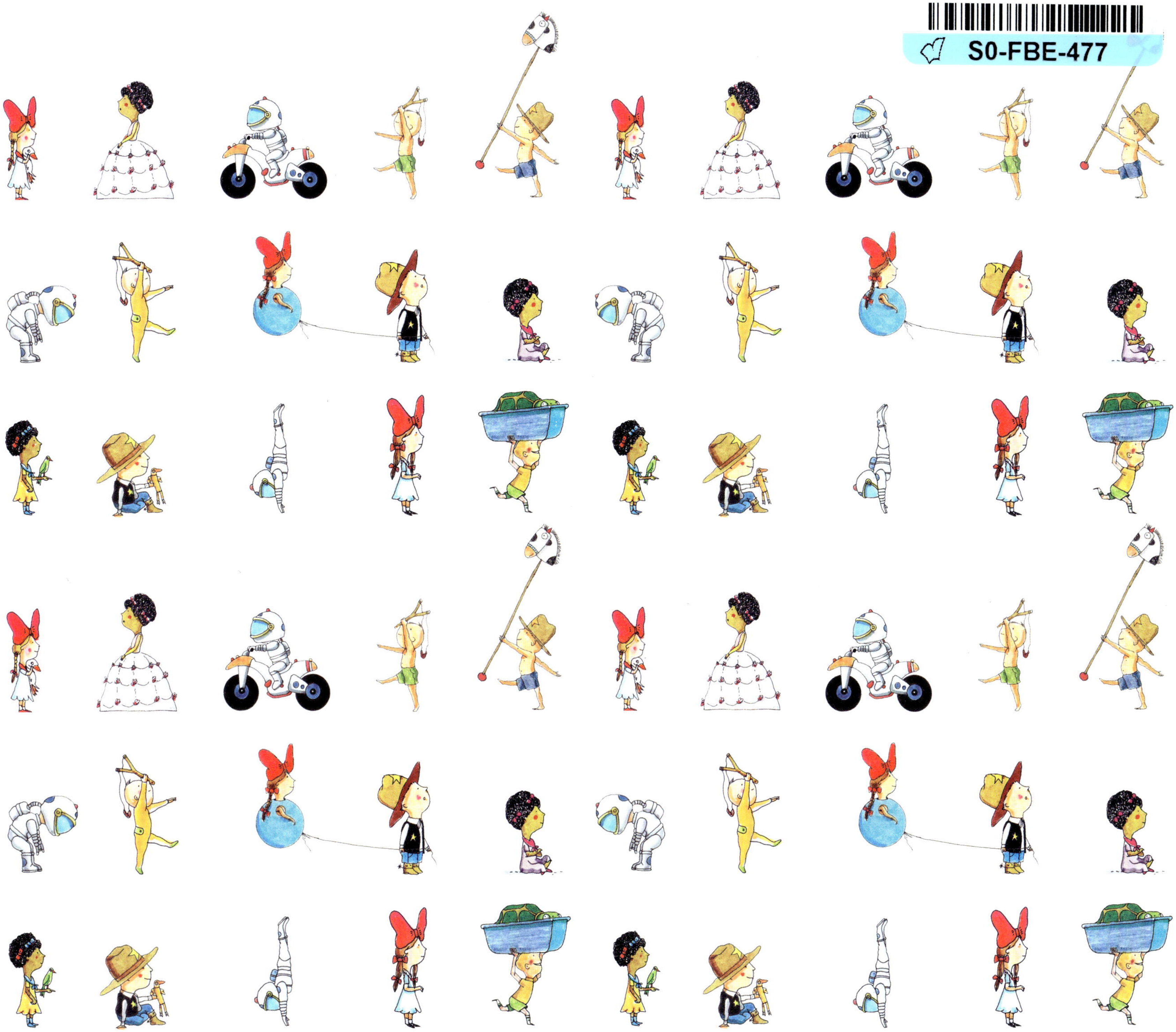

CUENTO DE LUZ

To my favorite people, for helping me to stay afloat.
—Sandra Alonso

To T. Ungerer and J. J. Sempé, who left us to draw in the clouds.
—Enrique Quevedo

This book is printed on **Stone Paper** that is **Silver Cradle to Cradle Certified®**.

Cradle to Cradle™ is one of the most demanding ecological certification systems, awarded to products that have been conceived and designed in an ecologically intelligent way.

Cuento de Luz™ became a **Certified B Corporation** in 2015. The prestigious certification is awarded to companies that use the power of business to solve social and environmental problems and meet higher standards of social and environmental performance, transparency, and accountability.

Auntie Maggie and Her Five Nephews and Nieces
Text © 2023 by Sandra Alonso
Illustrations © 2023 by Enrique Quevedo
© 2023 Cuento de Luz SL
Calle Claveles, 10 | Pozuelo de Alarcón | 28223 | Madrid | Spain
www.cuentodeluz.com
Original title in Spanish: *La tía Marita y sus cinco sobrinos*
English translation by Jon Brokenbrow
ISBN: 978-84-18302-67-1
1st printing
Printed in PRC by Shanghai Cheng Printing Company, January 2023, print number 1864-6
All rights reserved.

Auntie Maggie
and Her Five Nephews and Nieces

By Sandra Alonso * Illustrated by Enrique Quevedo

Like every other summer morning, Auntie Maggie set off for the swimming pool with her nephews and nieces:

Timmy, Tammy, Tommy, Tummy and Temmy.

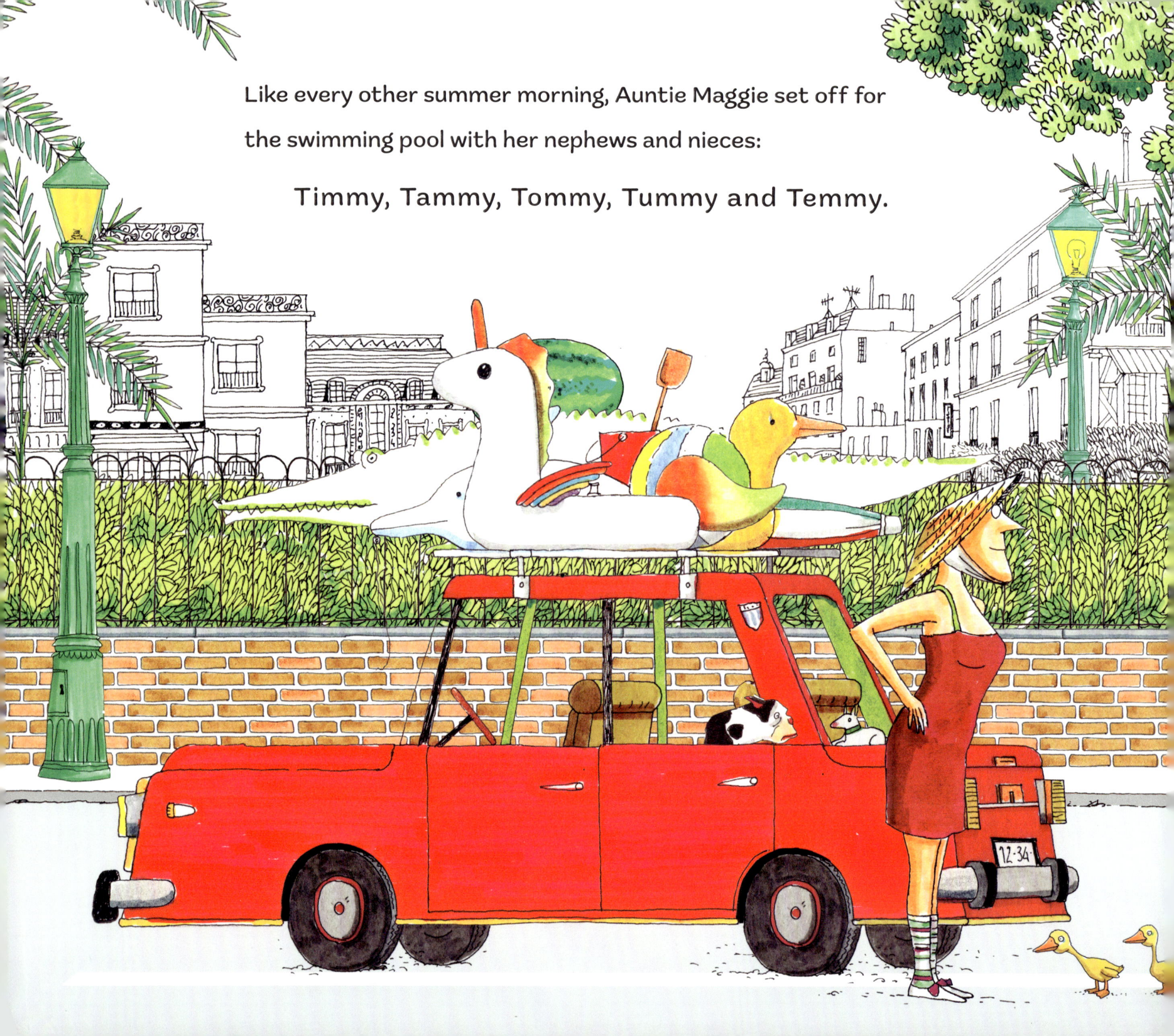

They spent the whole year waiting for summer to come so they could all enjoy these special days together.

Auntie Maggie was always the first one to get into the pool.

Timmy, Tammy, Tommy, Tummy, and Temmy usually took a little longer.

Timmy was the first of the children to reach the pool.

Just as he was about to dive in, he said,

"Oh no! I didn't bring my diving goggles!"

And so, she landed right on Auntie Maggie's back so she wouldn't swallow any water.

Tommy was the third of the children to reach the pool.

Just as he was about to dive in, he said,

"Oh no! I forgot to put on sunscreen!"

And so, he jumped right onto Auntie Maggie's back in the shadow of his brother and sister.

Temmy was the fourth of the children to reach the pool.

Just as he was about to dive in, he said,

"Oh no! I forgot to put on bug spray!"

Realizing he was surrounded by wasps, he jumped right onto Auntie Maggie's head.

It was a joke! She hadn't really forgotten anything. She just thought it would be fun to go along with her brothers and sister.

After Tummy jumped in, Auntie Maggie and her five nephews and nieces began to sink to the bottom of the pool.

She couldn't support the weight of all the children's problems...

She had to do something!

At home, while they were having a snack, she looked at Tummy, Temmy, Tommy, Tammy, and Timmy.

"You know, things round here have got to change...
Your Auntie Maggie isn't a life jacket!" she said in a serious voice.

And so, they got to work.

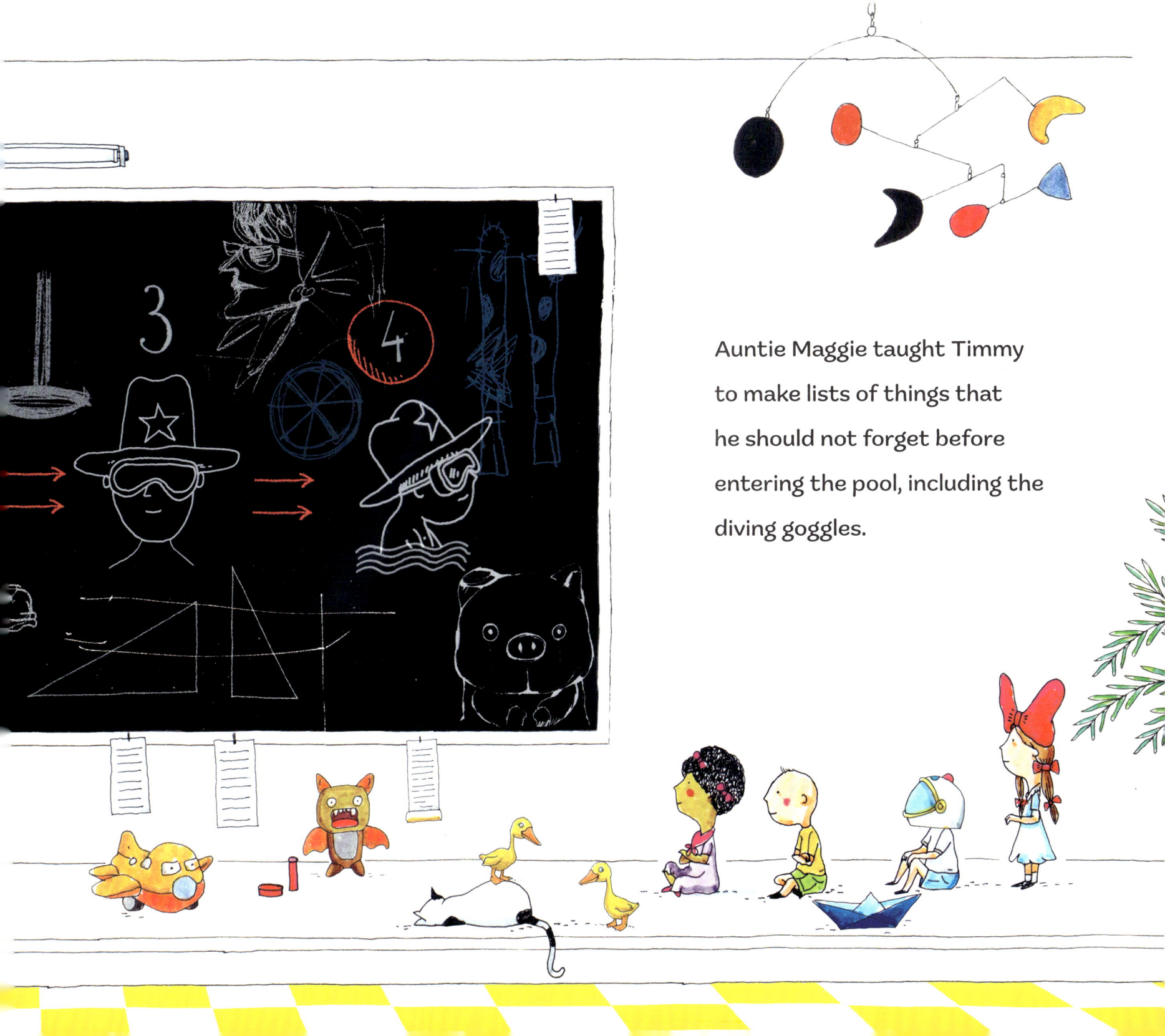

Auntie Maggie taught Timmy to make lists of things that he should not forget before entering the pool, including the diving goggles.

Auntie Maggie taught Tammy to swim so there wouldn't be a problem if she forgot her water wings again.

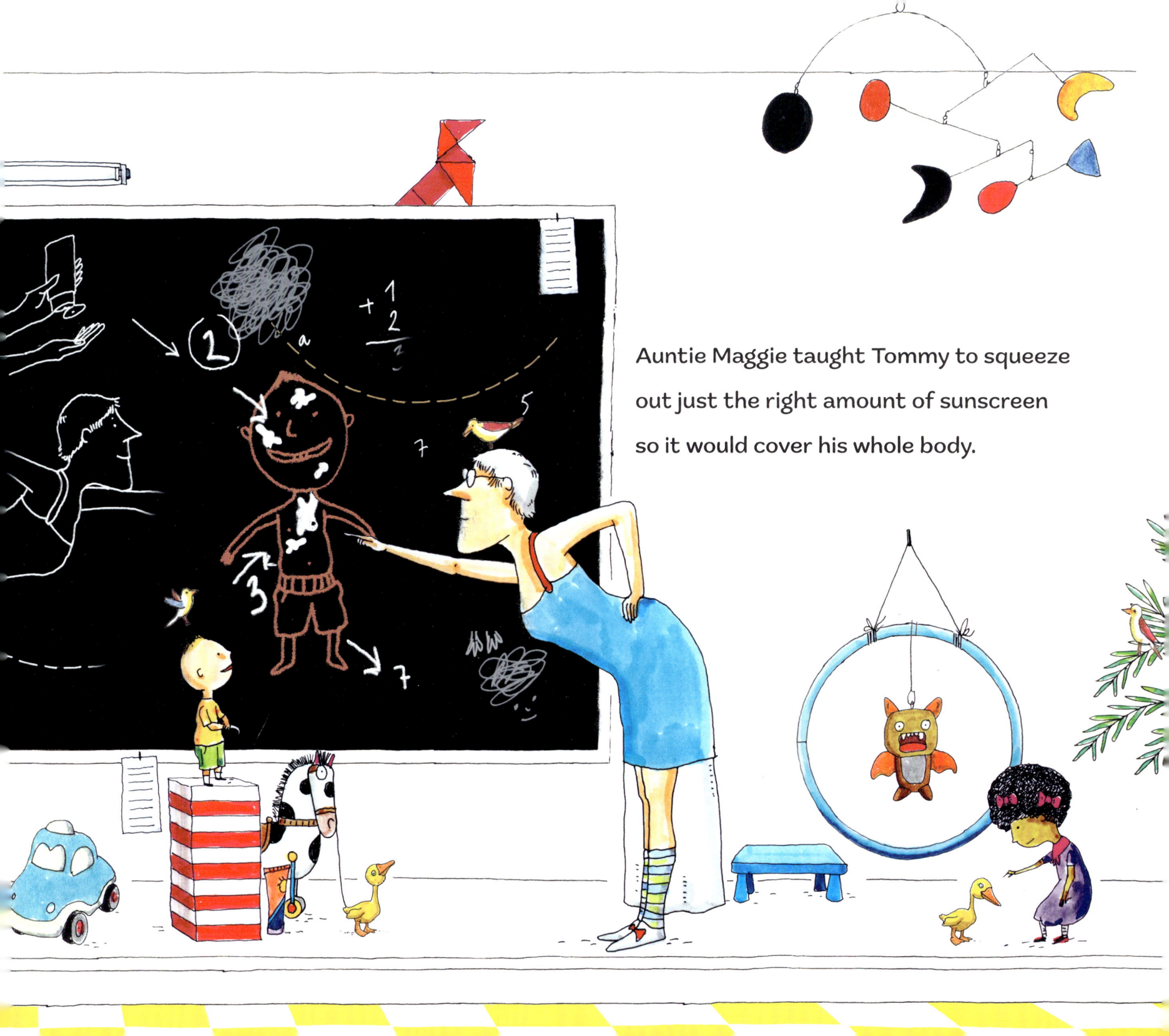

Auntie Maggie taught Tommy to squeeze out just the right amount of sunscreen so it would cover his whole body.

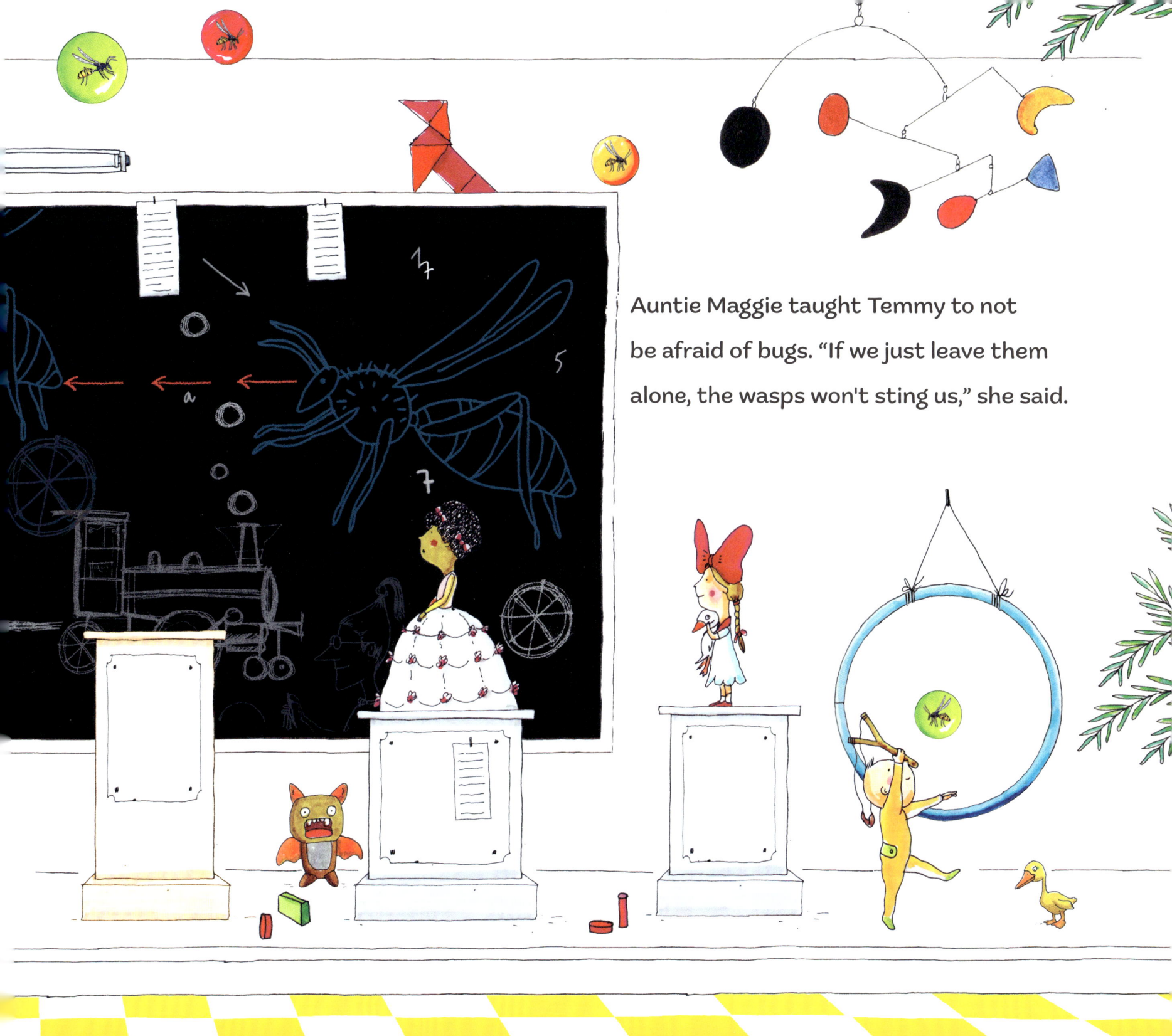

Auntie Maggie taught Temmy to not be afraid of bugs. "If we just leave them alone, the wasps won't sting us," she said.

Auntie Maggie taught Tummy ... she was only joking! She didn't have to teach Tummy anything ...

... because Tummy enjoyed just being with her brothers and sister and her aunt every day.

That day, they all understood that

it was easier to try to fix problems than to

keep carrying them around with you,

because they can often end up making you sink.

Auntie Maggie's five nephews and nieces began to ask her for help only when things got really complicated.